Boat Girl

Boat Girl

MARY COCKETT

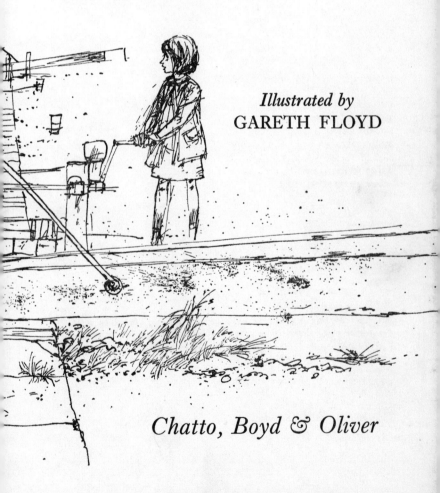

Illustrated by
GARETH FLOYD

Chatto, Boyd & Oliver

Published by
Chatto & Windus Ltd
40-42 William IV Street
London W.C.2

★

Clarke, Irwin & Co Ltd
Toronto

Some other books by Mary Cockett
ASH DRY, ASH GREEN
STRANGE VALLEY
TWELVE GOLD CHAIRS
SOMETHING BIG
THE WILD PLACE
ROSANNA THE GOAT
ANOTHER HOME, ANOTHER COUNTRY
FARTHING BUNDLES

© *Mary Cockett* 1972
First edition 1972

ISBN 0 7011 0476 7

Printed in Great Britain by
T. and A. Constable Ltd, Edinburgh

Contents

1

Mooring-rope

Gina yawned. She was still half asleep as she pedalled along the canal tow-path, but then it was only *five* o'clock in the morning. The creaking sounds of the ancient bicycle were loud in the quiet countryside.

Pressing harder on the pedals, she tried to hurry. Her father, patient man though he was, would expect the lock gates to be ready for him. Today in particular he was in a hurry because his elder son had a toothache, so awful a toothache that even George was willing to go to the dentist, and the sooner they reached him the better.

Gina half saw the pleasure-boat she was approaching, but she did not notice its mooring. A second later the rope caught her bicycle. As she was flung against a tree, she gasped with pain. The sound was not heard above the clatter of the bicycle as it dislodged itself from the rope and then crashed to the ground.

The cabin doors of the *Marybell* were jerked open, and a tousle-headed man and boy, both still in pyjamas, stepped out on deck.

'Great heavens!' said the man.

By the time they had put out the gang-plank, the boy's mother too had appeared, a coat over her pyjamas.

'Hold on!' Mr Weaver called to Gina. 'I'll help you.'

His wife stopped a yawn half-way through as she realized that it was she who was responsible for what had happened.

8

' What *have* I done ? ' she said, but nobody answered.

A pain was stabbing in Gina's forehead, and as she pressed on her foot in order to try to stand she winced.

' Steady, child,' said Mr Weaver. ' Don't stand on it. Let me take your weight. There now, just let yourself come sideways to sit on this tree stump. That's right.

Poor child ! Why didn't *I* look at that mooring-rope last night ! '

So far Timothy had said nothing. Now he caught sight of the time on his father's watch and said to Gina, ' It's terribly early to be out. Did you know it was only five o'clock, or did you get up early by mistake ? '

Dully Gina said, ' It isn't early for working boats.'

' O—oh ! ' said Timothy, excited as though he had met someone from another world. ' Are you from the narrow boats ? '

Gina nodded. It was strange, she thought, how shore people always looked at narrow boat people with curiosity, as though they were looking at creatures quite different from themselves.

The boy's mother was bending over her now.

' My dear, I'm bitterly sorry. I see now how stupid it was to tie up with the mooring-rope right across the tow-path. I didn't think. We're not used to boats.'

Gina said nothing. What was there to say ? Besides, she could see as she blinked away the tears that her own boats were approaching.

' I've got to see if the next lock gates are open. I've got . . . '

But the pain, when she tried to stand, was too much. She did not know *what* to do. Her father, at the tiller of the motor-boat, was drawing in behind the *Marybell*. Her mother, steering the engineless butty that he towed, could not see what was happening but she obeyed

10

his signal. On the cabin top of the butty Gina's dog, shaggy Old Bess, padded anxiously, waiting for her chance to set foot on the ground and find out what was wrong.

Mr Weaver said, ' I'm surprised your dog doesn't keep you company when you ride ahead on the towpath.'

Gina thought it was kind of Mr Weaver to talk to her just as he might have talked to anybody ' off the shore '. She was not as afraid to speak to him as she expected to be of shore people. It seemed easy to answer. ' Bess doesn't run much now she's old.'

' How old ? '

' Twelve.'

' She must be just about as old as you then.'

' Yes.'

Timothy had picked up the bicycle and propped it against a tree, an old rickety bicycle, with no gears, no bell, and, he noticed, worn brake-blocks. Not fit to ride really. He loosened the mooring-rope and stooped to fasten it to a low stump that was only an inch or two from the edge of the canal.

His mother said, ' If only I'd seen that stump last night ! '

' It was dark,' said Timothy, knowing she was in the wrong but wanting to shield her.

' Dark or not, I should have thought of danger to other people. It was stupid.'

Disgusted with herself, she said it all over again to Gina's parents, Mr and Mrs Lea, when they too had tied up. Old Bess had come fussing ashore, knowing that something had happened to Gina. She sniffed and snuggled against her, whimpering, trying to make up for whatever was wrong.

'Good Old Bess,' said Gina, rubbing her face for comfort against the shaggy ears.

The Leas were quiet people. They could have been angry; Mrs Weaver expected it, but they did not say much. They were getting used to the stupidity of shore people who took to the Cut for a holiday.

'Let me get a doctor,' said Mrs Weaver, 'to make sure there's nothing broken in that ankle. It's swelling already.'

'I expect she'll be all right,' said Mrs Lea. 'Gina's 'ad tumbles before. We all 'ave. Can't 'elp it sometimes in a life like this.'

'No, I suppose not.'

'It isn't long since my eldest broke 'is ankle when 'e fell against the edge of the Cut . . . oh, not 'ere where it's mud sides, further down where it's pile-driven.' Jerking her thumb at George, who was watching from the hatch, she added, 'And now 'e's got the toothache.'

Gina's other brother, Henry, stood half behind George, as usual. He was George's shadow, looked like him, and, like George, rarely spoke. Little Hetty, in cardigan and crumpled skirt, held tight to her mother's

12

apron. Their faces were masks—all except Gina's. They might have been sorry or angry or sad or worried, but it did not show. What showed on Gina's face was pain, around the mouth and in the dark eyes that peered below a curtain of near-black fringe.

'There's no call for a doctor,' Mrs Lea went on, ' no point in wastin' any more time.'

'We've got a load to deliver, you see,' said her husband, ' and we shall 'ave to take some time off for George to have 'is tooth out.'

'I have a suggestion,' said Mr Weaver. ' You take George to a dentist while we get a doctor to see Gina.'

'I'm not goin' to no strange dentist,' George called to his mother, ' only to 'im we saw before.'

That was a very long speech for George. He could go for hours without saying a word.

'You see 'ow it is,' said Mrs Lea. ' 'E'll only go to the one 'is father went to. Steady, Bess, don't push against Gina. Mind what you're doin'. Come now, lass.' She helped the hobbling girl towards the butty.

Mrs Weaver, unwilling to give in, kept alongside, saying, ' Suppose there's a broken bone and it sets wrongly. She might be lame.'

Surely, thought Timothy, a mother couldn't take a risk like that with her child. But Mrs Lea was not a woman to be persuaded, certainly not by a stranger off the shore. All she said in response was, ' Sister Mary'll 'ave a look at her.'

B

Mr Weaver asked, ' Who's Sister Mary ? '

At that there *was* some expression on the faces of all the narrow boat people. Fancy anybody *not* knowing who Sister Mary was !

' I've made a whale of a mistake, I can see,' said Mr Weaver.

Timothy felt embarrassed. When parents made mistakes it was worse than when children made them.

Mrs Lea's mouth had drawn itself into a thin line. It was bad enough that they had tied a strap across the tow-path, and now they did not know who Sister Mary was. That's shore people for you, she thought wryly.

' Sister Mary,' said Gina, ' has been the nurse for boat people as long as . . . ' She hesitated, and Mrs Lea filled in for her.

' She bandaged my knee when I was no older than our Hetty.'

She spoke almost in reverence, as Gina had.

' I see,' said Mr Weaver, but he did not.

' She lives further along.'

' We'll follow,' said Mrs Weaver.

Henry had gone ahead on the bicycle, and Gina lay down in the cabin of the butty. She looked at the chaos of tumbled blankets. It would have been her next job to take them off the side bed and off her parents' bed, and fold them away. Gina looked at Hetty's creased and slept-in clothes. Those shore people wore special clothes for sleeping in. Did all

shore people have them, she wondered ? She felt a
pang of envy, not the first, but the other times it had
not been clothes she had coveted. She envied them
first of all their confidence in themselves. A shore girl
had once said to her, ' You and your lot are ignorant
scum.'

Gina had not attempted defence. She felt herself
to be worthless. She never travelled on buses if she
could help it. She felt sick on buses, and not because of
the movement. She felt sick because it was such a
strain being with shore people, wondering what they
thought about her. She knew she was different, knew
that they knew she was different. *They* were educated,
whatever that meant. They had been to school for
years on end, so she thought they must be educated.
Her mother called it ' eddication ', and did not seem
to think much of it. Or was she jealous too ? Even
though she always said she never felt the need to read
and write ?

Gina's head ached and a bump was coming up under
her fringe.

Hetty was fretful, tired because she was bored, rubbing her greasy ringlets against Gina's lap. A shore
sister might have said nursery rhymes to her, but not a
boat girl. She did not know any. But that whining
made Gina's head ache more.

' If you'll pass the milk, Mum, I'll give her some,
then maybe she'll sleep.'

Slowly she swung herself to a sitting position, reached across the cabin and let down the cupboard door which now made a table. From the cabin top Mrs Lea passed the bottle of milk which kept cool in the breeze. ' It's back to tinned when that's finished,' she said.

2

Sister Mary

On the *Marybell* Mrs Weaver said, ' They were very decent to us. Even Gina didn't seem to bear us a grudge.'

' Hurry,' Timothy begged. ' Don't let's stop for breakfast.'

' No, we'll eat something as we go. It's the only way we'll be able to keep up with them. I expect they've had breakfast already.'

But there he was wrong. The Leas never had breakfast. They got out of bed, started up the motor and began the day. Time was money; the sooner they got the loads there, the bigger were their wages, and the sooner they could start back with another load. They had tea on the hob for much of the day, but not breakfast or any other meal to sit down to as a family all together.

' We're not keeping up with them,' said Timothy before long. ' Oh, you're *not* going to let that next pair of boats pass us, are you ? '

' This isn't a race track, Timothy.'

' Not the fairest remark I ever heard,' said Mrs Weaver.

' No, it wasn't,' said her husband with a laugh, for it was he who liked speed—on the road. ' But these are working boats, so they ought to have the lock first. This is their living.'

' I was thinking of you,' said Timothy, ' and how slow they'd be saying you were.' But then his attention was caught by a pigeon with a broad white band across its wings, a wood-pigeon, and it flew into a wood. Then immediately he saw a hedgehog curled up under a hedge. ' Both where they ought to be ! ' he said to himself, and the rightness pleased him. Hedgehog. Hedge pig. Was the nose like a snout ? Soon there was something else to take his eye, for a river ran into the canal and out again over two long flood weirs.

The idea for this holiday had been his, after seeing a film about inland waterways. He had come home full of envy of that person who had sat on the cabin top and, through binoculars, had seen a wide variety of birds. Timothy, on his visits to the country by car, would say, ' Couldn't you stop ? I think I've seen a—' But either they couldn't, or whatever it was had gone by the time they did. This summer they had no car. The old one had become too costly in repairs, and no good replacement had been found. So Timothy had had his wish—a holiday on one of the waterways man had dug through the countryside long ago, a holiday of moving on, to please his father, but movement of a kind that allowed Timothy the chance to see detail. It was always detail with Timothy—not just a field but the varieties of grasses, a tree rather than a wood, and even better the shape and colour of branch and leaf. Time to look and to see.

But now a flight of locks lay ahead, and there was work to do with the gates. So far Mr Weaver had not allowed Timothy to use the windlass, and *he*, having seen a lock-keeper with one finger missing after his first experience with a windlass, had not argued. Such a simple tool it was for opening the paddles, those doors deep in the lock gates. It released the gushing, pounding water that roared in his ears and thrilled and frightened him.

But if he did not use the windlass he was neat at leaping ashore, running up the lock steps and tying the thrown rope to a bollard. He enjoyed leaning his back against the balance beams and pushing the great gates open, especially when the beams were sun-warmed. But even for Timothy, as he opened the seventh pair of gates, the novelty had almost worn off. At the top of the flight of locks, they saw that they had caught up with Gina's boats.

' Thank goodness,' said Mr Weaver. ' I need a rest.'

' The family must be in one of those houses. We'll go ashore and wait.' An uneasy wait though, for a sense of guilt still nagged.

It was a quiet place. Trees. Tower of the village church. Old inn, a favourite with the boatmen for a hundred years. Mr Weaver reached for his camera. Almost opposite the inn were two tall cottages with, on one side, an ivy-covered house and on the other a high old mill that was a mill no longer.

The lock-keeper, as calm as the scene about him, weeded his garden beside the canal. The flowers were brilliant, fresher even than the new black-and-white paint on the balance beams. Timothy, on his father's instructions, went and sat on the near beam, and Mr Weaver said to the lock-keeper, 'Do you mind if we get you and your garden in the picture too?'

'W-ell,' said the lock-keeper, 'you're welcome, if you wish, but I'm no flower.'

'You look as if you belong in this picture.'

'I ought to, I've spent half my life here.' No sooner had the shutter clicked than he said, 'Oh, if only I'd thought! If I'd told you to wait a minute you might have got Sister Mary in it too. That really would have been a picture.'

Timothy said, 'The boat people made her sound special too.'

'I should say they would. She's given nearly a lifetime to nursing them, writing their letters, listening to their troubles. . . . Oh you must be the folks who tripped Gina with a mooring-strap. News travels on the Cut. You wouldn't think it, but it does.'

Then they saw Sister Mary coming. She was tiny and very old, but she stepped out lightly in her shiny black shoes. Long red cape. Navy overall, with the whitest collar and cuffs imaginable. From her head rose a starched head-dress, also startlingly white, and so like wings that Timothy felt a good puff of wind might lift her into the sky. There were laugh wrinkles round her eyes, but now she was talking seriously to his parents.

' So that's the situation. I can't tell for certain that there's nothing broken. If she goes, she'll try and walk on it. She's a determined little thing, and these boat families tend to struggle on regardless. They're brave —and foolish. And time is money to them. They don't stop if they can help it while there's a job to do.'

' But wouldn't you say the ankle ought to be X-rayed ? '

' I would, but Mrs Lea is all for " waiting and seeing ". They hate hospitals, so I know what that means.'

' Oh dear,' said Mrs Weaver. ' Suppose we took her by ambulance to the nearest hospital and then came back and followed their boats ? '

'You wouldn't catch them. They would go on longer than you could and start off earlier in the morning. They'll make up somehow for the time that's spent on getting George's tooth out.'

Timothy said, ' But they have to come back this way,

after they've delivered their load. We couldn't *miss* them.'

Sister Mary looked at his eager face, different from any boat child's. He was ready with suggestions and able to express them, as her dear boat people never could. 'That would mean having Gina on your boat for a day or two.'

' I'd like to do that,' said Mrs Weaver. ' We have a spare bunk as our daughter isn't joining us until after her camping holiday.'

' It's kind of you, but they don't hand over their children. I know you would like to make amends, but I doubt if Gina's ever spent a night away from her family in her life.'

The lock-keeper joined in. ' And you're shore people. She wouldn't know your habits.'

Habits ? Timothy was puzzled. What habits that would puzzle Gina ? What habits had they at all ?

His mother was saying, ' We'll make her feel at home, I assure you. Please, Sister Mary, persuade them to let her come with us.'

' Wait a minute then, and we'll see.'

Sister Mary walked to her door where the Leas were waiting.

The lock-keeper said, ' They won't consider it— unless Sister Mary actually orders it.'

' And then ? '

' Then they'll do it. Her word's law. With the

boat people she's got the power queens used to have over people in the old days.'

And Timothy was not surprised. She seemed to him to have something magic about her, and those eyes, bird-bright, missed nothing, he was sure. They would look, and see, and remember.

Before long she beckoned to them. What she had said to the Leas Timothy never knew, but she had got them to accept Mrs Weaver's suggestion. ' And Gina has agreed,' said Sister Mary. ' Haven't you, Gina ? '

Finding courage from the pressure of Sister Mary's hand, Gina gave a very small nod—not vigorous enough to wobble her fringe. To her mother she said, ' Will you bring me my things in my brown bag, Mum ? '

Timothy thought she meant her pyjamas and tooth-brush and so on, but the bag was a small paper carrier, surely too small for clothes.

As Mrs Lea gave it to Gina she said, ' Old Bess knows there's something wrong goin' on, and as for me I don't know what I'm thinking of, leavin' you 'ere.'

' Now, Mrs Lea,' said Sister Mary, ' don't make it harder for Gina. She will be well looked after, and I shall go with her to the hospital myself, along with Mrs Weaver.'

At the hospital Gina was glad of Sister Mary's familiar presence. She knew how to talk to the doctor as Mrs Lea would not have done. Gina looked round at the nurses' uniforms.

23

'Their caps aren't as nice as yours,' she whispered.
'Not so big and not so stiff.' And she was sure their
hands were not so comforting, but that she could not
bring herself to say.

The X-ray room seemed very strange to Gina, but
its machines did not worry her because Sister Mary

sat beside her, and she had promised that they would not hurt.

A voice said, ' Keep still now, still as a mouse. Hold your breath. Steady. . . . There now. Finished.'

Another wait and then the doctor was saying to Sister Mary, ' No break, I'm glad to say. It's sprained, but there's nothing that a few days' rest won't cure.'

He bound up the ankle so that the pain was less, and then ordered the ambulance to take them back to the canal.

3

The Tunnel

It was only when the ambulance men lifted Gina out at the tow-path that something near to terror came over her at being without her family and Old Bess. Up to that point Sister Mary had been with her, an accompanying angel. Any moment now that angel would be gone. And shore people always talked so much, and about so many things. Life on one canal was all Gina knew, and she could not think they would be interested. What was she to do? Whatever was she to do?

But now Mr Weaver was lifting her into the *Marybell*.

' Where would you like to be, Gina, on the top, or inside with your leg stretched out on a seat? '

' Inside,' said Gina. ' I'd only have to come down at the tunnel, so I may as well be in the cabin at the start.'

Timothy had been ordered to talk to Gina while his mother prepared a meal in the galley.

' Just talk,' his mother had said, ' and gradually she will feel at ease with us.'

' I wish Margaret had been here,' said Timothy.
' What shall I talk about ? '

' What a question ! From you ! Just start with
anything . . . with what you've been doing while we
were at the hospital.'

So Timothy babbled about canal exhibits which he
and his father had been seeing up in the old mill building which was now a canal museum. He talked about
the lanterns, about the big bonnets boat women used to
wear, about the kinds of twists and knots that are made
with rope on the stern of narrow boats. Gina hadn't
been into the museum, but she did know something
about knots. As Timothy rooted about for a length of
thick string so that she could demonstrate, Sister Mary
was waving and smiling from the tow-path. They
were away.

Gina began to look around her, at the smart fittings,
the bright cushions, the little curtains of modern design.
On her boat the curtains had been hand-made by her
grandmother, crocheted in white cotton according to
the customs of the boat people.

As Timothy laid the table he said, ' It must be a
squeeze for all six of you at meal-times. Where do you
all sit ? '

' Three eat at the table.'

' And the rest ? '

' Oh, anywhere, where they can. On the counter.
Anywhere.'

27

' The counter ? '

' Where the steerer stands on the motor. We don't generally stop to eat till night.'

' It must be difficult to talk, with you all scattered about and on two boats.'

As Gina made no reply, he said, ' I mean, at home we sit around the table for ages, just talking. There's always something—at my school, or Margaret's, or at my father's office. And now my mother's taken a part-time job interviewing people, and she's full of it. It's really livened her up.'

As he explained, it came clear to him that in his family they all had their different days. He hadn't thought till that moment how Gina's family were together all the time, all having the same sort of day. She was silent, and he was at a loss how to go on, but since she was looking round the cabin with interest, he said, ' Small, isn't it ? '

That remark surprised her into a reply. ' You've got a lot of space here.'

' That's funny. It doesn't feel much. It feels squeezed up after a house.'

' What's it like ? '

' What ? '

' Living in a house.'

Timothy's brow puckered. ' I don't know what to say. I was going to ask you about living on a boat all the time. That's what's interesting. I've never thought

28

about living in a house. I've lived in one all my life.'

' And you have friends ? And they live in houses ? '

' Or flats, yes.'

But she went on waiting, so he said, ' We have a dining-room, a sitting-room, and a nice bright kitchen that's always warm. Let's see, three bedrooms and a little room where my father develops his films, and a bathroom, and two lavatories, one up, one down. Garden, with flowers and vegetables and a lawn, and a hedge that always needs cutting. TV, two radios, record-player, a guitar we can't play much, and loads of books. I've got a big old arm-chair in my bedroom, where the train set used to be. I could never be bothered with that. Margaret's still got all her dolls and her dolls' house. Funny, that. Well, not really. I've still got my toy rabbit and one teddy. I collect stamps now. You ought to see some of them under the magnifying glass. Really super. The foreign bird ones are best. A boy at school brings me them. His father's a pilot.'

Gina listened to it all and would have gone on listening, but Timothy waited now for her to speak.

' I've been into a house a few times,' she said, ' but I've never spent a night there.'

' Never ? Never spent a night in a house ? ' Timothy was looking hard at Gina.

' No.'

' When you go for a holiday, where do you stay ? '

' We don't . . . go anywhere. We just tie up for a few days, that's all.'

' And sleep on your usual boat ? '

Gina nodded. Her head ached. As she touched the lump that had come up under her fringe, Timothy felt very sorry for her.

' It's a pity it isn't Margaret here instead of me,' he said. ' She'll think so too. After her camp, she'll be joining us. It'll be a surprise to find you here—if you're still with us.'

Gina had just begun to feel slightly comfortable with Timothy. He talked a lot and didn't seem to expect much in the way of replies. Now she felt nervous again at the thought of this girl she did not know. She hoped she wouldn't be there by then. Her father would be doing a quick turn-round after delivering his load. What she said was, ' Is she . . . is she very smart, your sister ? '

A great laugh was Timothy's answer. He called to his mother, ' Gina wants to know if Margaret is smart.'

' She can be when she likes.'

But Timothy said to Gina, ' She doesn't often like. She's all for old jeans and sweaters and sandals. Margaret, smart ! ' The idea still amused him, and he put his head out to tell his father who was at the tiller. But his father's face had an anxious look.

' What's the matter ? ' Timothy was at his side in a minute.

' Nothing really.   I was just thinking about the tunnel.'

The land on either side of the canal was rough, and on the right side steep.   A mass of brambles and tangly bushes stretched up the hillside.   A swan came gliding by, uttering encouraging noises to her one large cygnet. There was no other sound—no traffic noise of any kind, and nobody.

' Isn't it strange here,' said Timothy, ' as if there were no other people in the world ? '

But his father had no time for fancies, with a boat to navigate.   He was looking ahead at the huge green hill and the black gouge of the mouth of the canal tunnel. Somebody had had to cut that tunnel slap through the hillside without the aid of modern machines !

' I suppose you've been through here many times, Gina.'

' Dozens.'

' And you don't mind it ? '

' We don't take any notice of it.'

' No, I suppose not,' said Mr Weaver doubtfully.

' We have 'lectric light now,' she said, as though that solved everything.

Mr Weaver switched on his in readiness.   Imagine anybody having gone through with only lamplight.

His wife now sat opposite Gina in the cabin.

Gina said, ' Hasn't the captain a raincoat ? '

' Yes.   Why ? '

'He'll need it on in the tunnel if he isn't used to coming through.'

'Why? Are there drips?'

'More than drips when you come to the air shafts unless it's been very dry weather. You can dodge the water if you know how to rock the boat at the right minute.'

Rock the boat at the right minute ! Whatever did the child mean ? It sounded alarming. Child ! She was more like a little old woman.

Mrs Weaver passed her husband's coat out to him : ' Gina says you'll need this. It's wet in the tunnel.' It seemed better not to mention ' rocking the boat '. Mr Weaver slipped the coat round his shoulders and fastened the top button, saying, ' Go inside then, Timothy.'

Timothy went, willingly. In dismay he said to Gina, ' The tow-path stops at the tunnel.' It was a horrible discovery.

But Gina only said, ' Well, we don't need it.'

' No, *we* don't, but in the days when horses pulled the boats, where did the horses put their feet ? '

' They went up there,' said Gina, pointing up the hillside where there was a faint sign of a narrow path among the thistles and the brambles.

' By themselves ? '

' Oh no ! ' said Gina, beginning to be surprised at what shore people did not know. ' One person off the boat led the horse up the hill and over and down the other side, to where the tunnel ends.'

' Hm,' said Mrs Weaver. ' I think perhaps that person and the horse had the better bargain.'

Timothy thought so too, but there was nothing for it now but to go on. They were at the mouth of the tunnel, and now overhead, instead of the wide blue sky, an arch of brick enclosed them. They were in the tunnel and the world was left outside.

'Listen how different the noise of the motor is in here,' said Timothy, and his voice was raised. 'You hardly notice it outside. Look at the mud stalactites on the roof!' He had to keep talking to make the tunnel bearable. 'Look how the cracks in the brickwork show! A bit drippy, isn't it?'

'Ugh! Right down my neck,' said his father. But drips were nothing, as he was soon to know. 'It isn't so bad steering in here after all: not half as bewildering as I thought it might be, though I can't see far at a time.'

'It's eerie though,' called Timothy. 'Why are our lights flickering?'

As he spoke they flickered again twice—and went out. Blackness darker than pitch enwrapped them, but the boat surged on. Mr Weaver flicked the switch again but without result. Mrs Weaver stood up, knocking her head on a shelf.

Timothy called, 'I can't see anything at all.'

And then the *Marybell*, as if waiting only for that admission, seemed to seize the chance in the confusion to be evil. She banged into the right-hand wall, and the echo beat back and forth, dinning in their ears, and the motor alone was very loud. Water sloshed into the boat.

'Keep straight,' screamed Timothy.

'I was. I thought . . .' His father was frightened.

Never before had Timothy heard fear in his father's voice. ' I don't seem to . . . It's so dark I've no sense of direction . . . I don't know what's straight or where I'm— '

And the *Marybell* banged into the left-hand wall, and then back in a mad way to the first side.

' Father ! ' cried Timothy, and the echo wailed, shaking in the arched blackness, piercing up through the engine noise.

Then Mr Weaver, fearful of holing the boat, turned off the engine. Now, thought Timothy, they would never get out, never.

It was at that point in the panic that Gina, grasping both sides of the doorway, hobbled out of the cabin.

' Let me,' she said quietly, placing herself in front of the tiller and starting the motor again.

' Your foot ! ' Mrs Weaver protested, but only faintly.

The boat shuddered once more against the wall before Gina got her under control. Then the water stopped lashing and slapping, and the *Marybell*, like a wilful dog that feels the touch of a master, came to heel.

' Phew ! Good girl, Gina ! ' The relief in Mr Weaver's voice was very great. ' Good girl. This boat was completely out of hand.' He had scarcely recovered from the shock when from just ahead came the sound of pouring water. ' What's that ? '

' Water down the air shaft.' Gina's voice was calm. ' There's a high hill above us and a lot of water coming

35

through the earth. That's what you needed your coat for. Hold tight ! '

As she spoke she steered sharply to the left for a second only, rocking and tilting the boat round a cascade of water. A cup slid to the floor, but the *Marybell* had edged past the torrent.

' You *dodged* it ! ' said Mr Weaver with admiration.

' It's just a knack.'

' One worth having ! Is there another of those . . . air shafts ? '

' Yes, but I hope I shall be able to dodge it too.'

' You're a marvel. Thank God you were here.' Then, recalling what had caused her to be there, he thought how stupid his remark must have sounded.

Gina said nothing, for she did not know what to say. She had only done what seemed obvious to a boat girl, taken a hand when it was necessary.

They travelled slowly but steadily through the blackness. It did not seem easy to talk in that darkness, with the engine-sound battering back from the walls, but shouted talk was better than the silence in which Timothy and his mother were sitting.

' Are there always air shafts in tunnels ? '

' Not in short ones, but there has to be some air in long tunnels,' said Gina, 'or the fumes could kill people. I've heard tell they did one time, but I don't know if it's true.'

Then Timothy was startled out of his silence. ' I've

36

just thought of something awful! If the horse was taken over the top in the old days before there were engines, what got the boat through ? '

Gina answered in one word.

' Legs.' Then before Timothy could speak again, she said, ' Look out, another air shaft coming ! '

This time it was less of a shock. Another swerve and a tilt and they were past, splashed a little but that was all.

' Did you say *legs* got the boat through ? '

' That's right. Men called leggers got on the boats near Sister Mary's, and legged the boats through.'

' I don't see.'

Mrs Weaver said, ' I've read about this, I remember now. The leggers lay on their sides on a big plank that stretched across the boat, heads towards the middle, and feet out at the tunnel wall—and they pushed with their feet. Like lying-down walking it was, and the pushes sent the boat along.'

' Yes,' said Gina, thankful not to have to try to find the words.

' What happened at the other end ? '

' They just got off and brought the next boat back through the tunnel.'

' Phew ! What a terrible way to earn a living ! ' said Mr Weaver, wiping his brow, and it was not only water he tried to get rid of. It was a feeling of horror. ' Thank goodness those days are done.'

37

' They are mostly,' Gina agreed, ' but there is a place where my dad and George have done legging now and again when the boat's been travelling unloaded and too high in the water to bring through safely with the motor on.'

' And I thought of you just gliding along, peacefully, quietly ! '

' Mostly we do. It gets boring sometimes.'

Then Mr Weaver saw a welcome sight. ' Far ahead ! Is that really *daylight* ahead ? '

It was some time since Gina had seen a pinpoint of light grow into a small blur, but she had not thought to mention it. Nothing of this was new to her. The failure of the electric light had been a tiresome nuisance but to her nothing more. She felt quite matter-of-fact about that glimmer: it would slowly grow larger and larger until it showed itself for what it was, the far end of the tunnel.

But when Timothy heard the mention of daylight he had to squeeze out beside his father to see it for himself.

In the voice of one who witnesses a miracle, he said, ' Light ! '

The glimmer of grey took shape more and more until it was firmly outlined by the tunnel's arch.

' I never thought I'd like the sight of slimy brick-work,' said Mr Weaver.

His wife pointed into the water as they almost reached

the outdoor world. 'A water-rat swimming,' she said, and her voice was gentle.

' I thought you hated any sort of rat,' said Timothy.

' I do, but to see *anything* is a pleasure at the moment.'

' I agree,' said Mr Weaver. 'And now, Gina, go in and rest that leg. Fancy the invalid having to come to the rescue ! What we should have done without you I shiver to think.'

As she handed over the tiller Gina said, 'You'd have got your bearings in another minute.'

' I very much doubt it.'

' So do I,' said Timothy. 'You were super, Gina ! Daylight ! Isn't it marvellous ! And the blue of those flowers, look, periwinkle. And the grass—the greenness ! ' He gazed round as though seeing the world for the first time. His mother was trying to thank Gina and not knowing how to thank her enough.

' It was nothing,' said Gina, and she meant it, but the praise from this shore family wasn't nothing. It helped her as nothing else could have. She would find it easier to be with them now that she had proved to herself that there was something she was good at and they were not. She felt less the odd one out than she could ever have thought. If only they would keep to the subject of canals, she would be able to talk.

They went on to speak of the painting of castles and roses on some of the narrow boats, and on the gay, painted water jugs and ' dippers ', and of the plates with lacy edges which had belonged to Mrs Lea's grandmother.

' It's the brasses I like,' said Timothy.

' I agree they're lovely,' said his mother, ' but the polishing ! '

' That's just it ! ' said Gina. ' They're one of my jobs, and they don't stay bright for long, especially in rainy weather. I like the old lantern and the brasses the horse used to wear, but I don't like the brass knobs my mother collects, and it just annoys me to have to polish the brass rails on the side by the stove.'

' Why them in particular ? ' asked Timothy.

' Because we're always having to hang damp things on them and then the shine goes—damp tea-cloths, or damp blankets.'

' Damp blankets ? '

' The walls get damp with steam, and then it runs down on the bed-clothes. We don't get them rained on. We keep the hatch closed.'

' Isn't it stuffy then ? ' asked Timothy, whose bed-room window was always open.

' I don't know,' said Gina, who had never slept any-where else. ' Sometimes, if I've slept extra badly, I wait till my mum and dad start off and then I climb into their bed and sleep all morning perhaps, with the fresh air coming in. I don't like my side bed.'

' You mean that narrow seat opposite the stove is a bed at night ? '

' Yes. And it's too short for me now. Narrow! I fell off once on to Old Bess. It gave her a shock, and me too.'

She laughed, but Mrs Weaver did not feel like laughing. A bed too short and too narrow to turn on.

Gina was smiling, relaxed and surprisingly happy. She had never felt relaxed and able to talk to shore children on the way to school, and she wasn't with them *at* school. The canal children had their own room, and their own cloakroom. Those shore children nearly all had nice clothes, and shiny hair, and neat unbroken shoes. And how they chattered among themselves! But not to the canal children. *They* looked the odd ones out, and neither side knew what to talk about to the other, but to Gina it seemed that only her kind did not know what to say. She had heard a rumour that the canal children might have to share in the classes of the shore children, whose school it really was. She hoped it was only a rumour, or so far off that she would have left school before it happened. How could she, with her very little schooling, take her place in class with children of her own age? It did not bear thinking about.

4

Her Turn to Read

The *Marybell*'s lights were easy to mend in the day-light, and there were no more anxious moments for Mr Weaver at the tiller. Timothy took a short turn on a long straight pound. A 'pound' was Gina's word—the proper word—for the stretches of canal between locks. In the evening the countryside seemed very still. A frog croaked now and again, a fish plopped, some small creature rustled the hedge as it passed through, but that was all. No man-made din, especially no aeroplanes, Mrs Weaver noted.

After supper she took down a book. Her husband sat doing a crossword, but ready to lend an ear too. Timothy sat waiting while she turned the pages. Then she looked across at Gina.

'We only started this story yesterday evening, Gina. I'll tell you what's happened so far, and then I'll go on.'

Gina sat and listened, without showing any of the surprise she felt. She had heard her teacher read stories, but she had never imagined that a mother might read to her family.

And it was not only Mrs Weaver who read. After a while she handed over the book to Timothy, pointing to the next paragraph. As one well used to it, he went on with the reading aloud.

The cabin was warm and comfortable. The supper had been nice too, different. Gina's ankle no longer burned, and she began to feel that this must be a holiday.

Timothy passed the book to his father next, but Mr Weaver said, ' Let Gina have her turn first.'

At that the joy dropped out of Gina's evening. A feeling of panic took its place. She hadn't even time to refuse. The book was already on her knee, and Timothy's finger was pointing. ' There,' he said.

Almost instantly they all realized that something was wrong. Gina twisted away from the book, hunched, holding her hands close to one side.

Mrs Weaver leaned forward and took the book away, saying, ' You don't have to read if you're feeling shy. We've always done it, but less recently because Margaret complains that reading aloud makes it too slow. Does it remind you too much of school ? '

' I like school,' said Gina, defending herself and her teacher, ' but I can hardly ever get there.'

' Why not ? ' Timothy's eyes were round.

' Well, how can I ? We're always on the boats, always on the move except when we're being loaded and unloaded.'

' Oh.' Did she really mean she didn't go to school ?

' Last trip there was something wrong with the motor. We were tied up at the depot, so I had three whole days at school.'

' I thought you were going to say three weeks.'

' Oh no ! ' said Gina, thinking longingly of something unattainable. ' One day in three weeks is about what we can manage, so we don't get on very fast. And we're all in one class for lessons, all ages together.'

' Oh, I shouldn't like that,' said Timothy firmly, ' big and little all in one form. How many of you ? '

' Sometimes twenty, sometimes two or three.'

' How very difficult for you ! ' said Mrs Weaver.

' And for the teacher.'

' Yes, it isn't her fault we're not much good, but I can read some things. Some can't that are older than me.'

Only then did Timothy realize that she might not have been able to read at all. Everybody he had met in all his life could read, he was sure of it. And Gina was two years older than Timothy, the same age as Margaret.

' I have a book of my own,' said Gina, leaning over to reach her small, brown carrier-bag. ' I keep *my* things in this, and I hang it up so that Hetty can't get at it.'

She seemed to want to prove that she had some possessions, especially such a scholarly thing as a

44

D

book. Out of the bag came Number Two of a soft-backed book with a pattern that Timothy recognized immediately. 'Oh but that's—' Then he stopped and mercifully his mother filled the gap quickly.

'They're a very good set to learn from,' she said. 'Margaret and Timothy both had them.'

The danger of embarrassment was past. But a sigh escaped the girl. Mrs Weaver leaned forward and put her hand over Gina's.

'Never mind about taking a bit longer to learn to read. You will learn in time, and there are other things in life.' Gina wanted to move the hand. She wasn't used to tenderness. 'My goodness, I shan't forget in a hurry the way you piloted this boat through the tunnel.'

'That was nothing,' said Gina, fiercely to keep the tears at bay. 'Anybody could do it with practice.'

'It's the same with reading.'

Timothy said, 'I like books, but I think I'd rather be able to take charge of a boat the way you did. I was scared stiff till you took over.'

But Gina was sure he was only being kind.

She said, 'I'd rather be able to read—and write. Some boaters say their children can write when they only mean they can *copy*. I'd like to be able to write down what I think—in a letter. I'll never be able to do that. I'll never be able to write a letter.'

Her sadness spread like a mist through the little cabin.

' But can't any of the canal children read and write—easily, like ordinary children ? ' asked Timothy.

' A few can—those who've had long spells tied up at the depot if their mother was ill or something. Then the children could go to school every day. And some who go to the hostel at the other end can read and write better than I ever will.'

' A hostel ? ' said Mr Weaver. ' They live there and go to an ordinary school every day ? '

' That's right, but mostly they only get into the bottom classes and the work's very hard for them. And the classes are too big for the teachers to bother with them much.'

' Better than only having a day at school every now and then,' said Mrs Weaver. ' If you'd so much like to go to school every day, why don't you go to the hostel ? '

' Me ? '

' Yes.'

' My mum wouldn't let me.' There plain, there pat, came the answer.

' Why not ? '

' Well, we're not overcrowded, with the two cabins to sleep in. Some boaters *have* to send some of their children if there's overcrowding.'

' Are you sure your mother wouldn't let you go ? '

' Yes. She says she don't need nobody to help her to look after her children.'

' But that isn't. . . .' Mrs Weaver stopped.

' Besides,' said Gina, ' I'd . . . I'd be frightened.'
There, now the words were out.

' To go away from home ? '

' Yes.' It was a barely audible sound, but her shame
was boundless.

' But you'd come back for the holidays, like children
at boarding-schools, and I expect parents can visit the
hostel ? '

' Oh yes, every two or three weeks when the boats
come up.'

' Well then ? '

' My mum wouldn't let me, and . . .' She paused,
but one confession had made the next easier, and the
words came out in a rush. ' I don't think I'd like it.
You have to do as you're told in the hostel, and pretty
quick, and you have to help with the washing-up and
that sort of thing. That's what they say.'

' So what ? You help on the boats. Look at the
time you spend polishing brass, peeling potatoes, looking after your little sister, helping with the gates—or
steering while your mother does those jobs.'

' Oh yes, we work a lot. But we'd be more bored if
we didn't.'

' Fancy steering a boat that stretches from one end
of a lock to the other ! ' said Timothy.

' We're not supposed to, but we do. It's nothing
really,' said Gina.

' Timothy thinks it is,' said Mr Weaver. ' We all rather take for granted what we can do, but to other people it looks special.'

He was as sorry for Gina as his wife was, and already growing fond of her. The girl looked at him with dog-like attachment as if amazed that he, an adult and a shore person, should bother to talk to her as though she mattered.

' About this hostel,' said Mrs Weaver. ' Surely you needn't mind doing as you're told and helping a bit ? Lots of children who go to boarding-schools make their beds and wash up and so on. I shouldn't let that be a worry.'

' You're not free at the hostel,' said Gina, with the look of a wild bird caged. ' You're not *free*.'

Mrs Weaver felt like saying that nobody was exactly free, that it wasn't freedom to have to go up and down a waterway year in, year out.

But she only said, ' I expect you mean there are rules in the hostel, and that you're not allowed to wander wherever you like ? '

' Yes.'

' Well, there have to be some rules where a large number of people live together. You wouldn't really mind, and it's not for ever.'

Timothy said, ' Even in our *house* there are rules.' Ticking off the items with his fingers he started: ' I have to clean my teeth night and morning, polish my shoes twice a week, make my bed at week-ends and in the holidays, wash up the breakfast things on Saturdays and Sundays, mow the lawn. . . .'

' Oh, Tim, stop ! '

' I'm just saying.'

His mother turned again to Gina. ' You're sure it's not the cost of your being at the hostel that would make your mother refuse ? '

' We don't have to pay.'

' You don't ? Who does then ? Somebody must.'

' The education people,' said Gina. ' Well, that's what I heard. I don't know why they do it. I don't know who they are. We're supposed to have another set of clothes besides those we go in, but not everybody does. And we're supposed to have pocket-money, but that's all it costs.'

' Oh, Gina,' said Mrs Weaver urgently, ' it seems to me you're missing a chance here.'

' You're interfering, my dear,' said Mr Weaver.

' I know. Somebody must. It's as clear as daylight that canal trade is getting less. Working life on the canals—working on the boats people live on—can't go on much longer. You must have heard, Gina, that the fleet may be sold ? '

' Nobody's told me, but I've heard talk. My mum doesn't believe it, but my dad told her it was because she didn't want to believe it. It's the only life she knows or wants to know.'

' But he—your father—what will he do if the boats stop ? '

' Well, there are private companies. Or else he might do painting jobs at some boat yard or the docks. He's done painting at the depot when we've been held up there.'

' Then you'd live in a house,' said Timothy, ' and have friends down the street and go out together.'

But Gina shook her head. ' No house. My mum wouldn't ever leave the water. We'd tie up near some docks and live on the boats and pay rent, I suppose.'

' So, you see, your parents have been thinking about life changing on the canals. I'll tell you what, Gina. More and more people are taking canal holidays, and they have to be taught how to manage their boats. You'd be marvellous at that. You know it all already. And boats have to be cleaned between one set of holiday-makers and the next. And in the winter and spring you could help in the office—booking the holidays and so on. There could be stewarding work, too, on the bigger boats where people just want to be passengers.'

Gina looked as though someone was unrolling a picture on paper she had thought to be blank.

' You like the idea, don't you ? ' said Timothy.

' Yes, I like it, but do . . . would they have girls in these jobs ? '

' Oh, yes,' said Mrs Weaver. ' We booked our holiday through a girl of about twenty, and it was she

51

who showed us round the boat. Another girl gave my husband what you might call a driving lesson. Two or three would have been better.' She grinned, but her husband chose to ignore the remark.

He said, ' Aircraft stewards are girls too, all those I've seen anyhow. Oh, don't worry, Gina, we're not trying to send you up in the air, just pointing out that girls do such jobs.'

Mrs Weaver turned the conversation back where she thought it should go. ' But if the boats are sold, the hostel will close, I imagine. There wouldn't any longer be a reason for it, would there ? '

Gina got the drift of that at once, for she said, ' So it's now or never, isn't it ? '

' Well, fairly soon. But if you were to go to the hostel, and if you found you really didn't like it, you could leave, you know.'

' Could I ? Without a lot of trouble ? '

' Certainly. You wouldn't be kept there against your will.'

' No. It's not a prison. I don't mean you'd just walk out, but the arrangement wouldn't be difficult to make. The matron or warden would get in touch with your parents.'

Gina's face was solemn. She had never seriously considered the hostel before, but from that moment it was often in her thoughts.

' I'll have to see,' she said. ' I'd like to be the same

as other people.' She paused to put her book in the bag.

' You mean you'll go if your mother'll let you ? '

' I'll have to see,' said Gina again.

The little carrier-bag tipped sideways and something fell out. Before she could swing herself round to reach it, Timothy picked it up.

' It's an ear-ring,' he said, perplexed. ' *Very* fancy ! Yours or your mother's ? '

' Mine,' she said. ' They're for my eyes.' Her ears were pierced, and she slipped the ear-rings into position.

' Your *eyes* ? '

' To do them good. They say if you wear ear-rings it saves you getting eye-strain and having to wear glasses.'

' Surely it couldn't ? ' said Timothy, puzzled.

There was a strange silence in the cabin. Mrs Weaver had heard the old wives' tale without knowing anyone still believed it. It was Gina who broke the silence. Her face clouded over at a memory.

' I may not wear them again outside. Last time somebody in the street pointed and called out " Dirty boater ". We often get shouted at. How do they know we're off the boats when we're in a town ? '

Mrs Weaver thought of the dreary out-of-fashion clothes and Mrs Lea's ear-rings, and the black hair worn plaited and close to the head, but she only said, ' Perhaps it's because of the ear-rings if a lot of your people wear them. One doesn't usually see children in ear-rings.'

' We have seen some,' said Timothy, meaning to be kind, ' those three gypsy children who came to the door selling pegs, don't you remember ? '

An angry flush spread over Gina's face. To be linked with gypsies in any way at all was to the boat people the worst insult.

' We're nothing to do with gypsies, nothing. They're *lazy*. We do regular work all the year round.' Gina looked at the door as if she would like to go through it.

' I like gypsies,' said Timothy. ' I didn't mean . . .'

' Nobody doubts that you work,' said Mrs Weaver.

' Nobody,' agreed her husband. ' All those loads up and down the canal ! I don't know half enough about what you carry. What is it this trip ? '

' Timber,' said Gina, cheering up a little. ' I like it when we carry timber. I like the smell of wood. I like wheat too, especially the sound as it comes down the chute when we're being loaded.'

She talked on. Here she was, having a real conversation, with people who wanted to listen. Then, at a pause, after a long time, Mr Weaver looked at his watch and said, ' Ten o'clock already ! I can't think when I last had such an interesting evening. The time's flown, but we all ought to be settling down for the night if we're to have an early start.'

While Mrs Weaver helped Gina to get to bed,

Timothy and his father went out into the moonlight. A low mist had spread over the fields, a ribbon of white mist close to the ground. A horse was visible but it looked as though it swam, for the mist hid its legs and rose up to its shoulders.

Inside, Mrs Weaver was saying, ' Did you remember a nightdress ? ' Gina shook her head. There was no toothbrush in her bag either, for she did not possess one, but, as with the nightdress, Mrs Weaver assumed that the toothbrush had been left behind by mistake.

' Never mind. I'm not surprised you forgot after the shock we gave you. We have a spare pair of pyjamas here for Margaret, so you can borrow those. You're about the same size.'

Gina took them carefully as though they were precious. She did not say she had not forgotten hers, that she never had any special clothes to wear in the night. It was strange to go to sleep without Old Bess down there below her hand. In fact never in her life had she been away from Old Bess or her family for a single night, but she slept.

5

'Stemmed Up'

The next morning was fine and mild, and the grey-green waterway stretched ahead more like a river than a canal. There were no roads to be seen. They were there all right now and again above the neat rounded hump of a canal bridge, but there was no roar of traffic. The tow-path, except for the strip down the middle, was clover-covered. Here and there the water had sucked away a bit of land, and the tow-path had had to take itself further round.

'Peaceful!' said Mr Weaver, forgetting the din and panic in the tunnel. 'And millions of us work in dirt and noise in the cities. White foxgloves among the marguerites, and water-wagtails just skimming the surface.' He sighed with pleasure. 'This is how a holiday should be. Are you enjoying yourself too, Gina?'

'Yes.'

Only one word, but she meant it. Her ankle hurt less. It has been worth the hurt, she was thinking, just to sleep in those pyjamas, and then to sit at a table and

drink coffee and eat sizzling hot bacon and tomatoes in
the morning. She sat now on the cabin top in the sun.
Yesterday she would not have admired Mrs Weaver's
crisp red blouse and smart jeans. The boat women
did not wear trousers and thought ill of shore women
who did, but Gina almost liked them. Normally she
never gave a thought to clothes, but this morning she
was almost wishing she had something different from
her drab cotton dress that had lost its fresh colours
before it came her way. She had felt almost tempted to
stay in bed so that she could go on wearing those
pyjamas: it was a pity they got creased with being
slept in.

' Does it seem odd to have nothing to do ? ' Mrs
Weaver asked.

' Yes, it does a bit.'

' Can you play dominoes ? '

' Yes.'

' Well, we have some by mistake. I brought this
playing-card box thinking it had the patience cards in
it. I thought they might be useful if it rained.'

' Rain's the worst thing,' said Gina, sounding, as
often, older than she was. ' When it rains for days we
don't know what to do.'

' But you go on, I suppose ? '

' Oh yes. Just sitting in the cabin.'

While Mr Weaver piloted the boat Timothy and
Gina played dominoes on a tray. Gina concentrated

on the game, but Timothy's eyes were everywhere. All this countryside was new to him, and there on the tow-path striding out in a determined fashion was a mother hedgehog, with two young ones striving to keep up.

' Just look ! ' he said, his face full of wonder. ' Oh, they're stopping.'

But Gina wondered at him more than at the hedge-hogs. Already that day he had seen and been able to name more birds than she had ever noticed on all her journeys on this same route. And he found a joy in seeing and in recognizing. It wasn't only birds either. He lived in a town, but he knew the names of trees too. He hadn't been taught them at school either, for that she had asked him. Books, he had said, his own and books borrowed, it seemed, from somewhere called a library.

' What have they found ? We'll see in a minute.'

' It's egg,' said Gina. ' I can see the yolk running.'

' A hen's egg, do you think ? Or a pigeon's ? Or what ? '

' I don't know.' What a lot of questions, she thought.

Along the tow-path towards them rode a man on a bicycle. As he passed the *Marybell* he called to Gina, ' Got yourself a new family, eh ? '

Gina smiled.

He called again, ' I hear that dog of yours is missing you.'

And he was gone. At his words the smile had gone

from Gina's face too. Now she felt almost wicked to be enjoying herself without Old Bess.

Timothy broke into her thoughts without knowing how turbulent they were.

' Who was he ? '

' A lock-keeper, and he's a lengthsman too.' Then she saw that Timothy didn't understand. ' He's like an inspector for this section of the canal.'

' What is there to look for ? ' said Timothy, thinking of the inspection of track along a railway.

' Oh, to see that the water-level's right and the locks in order.'

' That's a nice job just pedalling along the tow-path.'

' Nice in the sunshine,' said Gina. But last winter there had been ice on the tow-path, and ice sealing all the parts of the lock gates that were generally movable. Every step up to every lock had been treacherous with ice. But she said nothing.

' Wake up, Tim. Another lock,' said Mr Weaver, as his wife took his place at the tiller.

As the bow of the *Marybell* entered the lock, Mr Weaver, with Timothy close behind, leapt ashore with the rope, or ' strap ' as he had now learnt to call it. He ran up the steps and wound the rope quickly round the bollard so that the boat stopped before it could crash into the upper gates. He was skilled by now at leaning his back against the balance beams and stepping backwards, opening the gate.

Over the small noise of the engine he called to Gina,
' I still feel I must be as strong as a giant to be able to
move gates as big as these.'

Gina's smile was that of a grown-up who watches a
child's pleasure at having learnt to do some ordinary
thing.

As they left the lock, she said, ' Once I got left behind
when I was steering the butty. The snubber broke.'

' The . . . ? '

' The rope that tows the butty. It just broke.'

' Didn't you shout ? ' asked Timothy.

' I tried,' said Gina, ' but there was an aeroplane
going over at the time, and I couldn't.'

' Like shouting in a dream ! ' said Timothy. ' Awful !
You need to scream and you open your mouth and no
noise comes out.'

' Just like that. But then my dad turned round and
saw me. I suppose the pull felt different.'

They were moving up to a bend which swept widely
round. On the left was a huge area of reeds and bul-
rushes. Coming down was a pair of narrow boats
laden with coal. The captain of the motor blew on his
hooter and gave a signal with his hand.

But Mr Weaver took it as a greeting and hooted and
waved in return.

' Hold out, Mr Weaver,' said Gina with an urgency
in her voice.

' Hold what out ? '

'Quick! He means, go on the side where there
isn't the tow-path.'

'Hold out? O.K.,' he said, signalling his willingness
and starting to obey, but asking Gina, 'Why me over
there?'

'He's got a big load, and he needs the deeper water
on the tow-path side.'

'Oh, what a lot I don't know!'

E   61

'What's the opposite of "hold out" then?' asked Timothy.

'"Hold in",' said Gina, and they all laughed.

Mrs Weaver said, 'We seem to be getting free education all the way with you on board, Gina.'

But the girl was concentrating. 'Don't go too far over in case you get "stemmed up"—stuck in the mud. Too far! He doesn't need all that space.'

'"Stemmed up" sounds very sticky,' said Timothy, enjoying the expression.

As the narrow boats passed, the woman on the butty called, 'You all right, Gina?'

'Yes, I am, thank you.'

'That's good. They've tied up so's George can have his tooth out.'

A scrap of news transmitted in passing and that was all. No time to talk, thought Mrs Weaver. 'Don't you ever stop to have a talk, Gina?'

'Oh no, not on the job. It would be wasting time. Only when we're tied up.

'You make me feel very lazy. I love being able to stop and chat with my friends.'

Timothy was gaping with admiration at the Turk's Head on the disappearing butty. It was complicated plaiting, and the rope was startlingly white.

'I wish I could do those marvellous patterns,' he said. Mr Weaver turned to look, but the *Marybell* proceeded, Turk's Head notwithstanding.

Gina had been sitting with her back to the way they were going. Now, as Mr Weaver turned, she felt the engine slow. She twisted round. The reeds were very near.

' Quick ! ' she cried, but she was too late.

' Stemmed up ! ' said Timothy laughing. But it was no joke to Gina.

Mr Weaver blew through his lips and said, ' I'm not very good at this job.'

' It's *my* fault,' said Gina fiercely.

' Indeed it isn't.'

' I should have watched you better.'

' I should have watched for myself. We'll be off in a minute, you'll see. There, with the engine in reverse, off we'll go.'

But they did not go.

' Nothing's happening.'

' No. We're stuck.'

' Stemmed up,' said Timothy. ' That's the right word on the Cut.'

' Never mind about words. You come here, Tim, and put her into reverse while I use the boat-hook.'

Timothy slid down and did as he was told, glad to be given something to do. Mr Weaver used all his strength on the boat-hook, but the *Marybell* stayed snugly where she was.

' As comfortable as a hippopotamus,' said Timothy.

' And no hope of a tide to float her off,' said Mrs

Weaver. 'Let's see if my weight on the boat-hook makes any difference.'

But the boat-hook might have been a knitting-needle for all the notice the *Marybell* took.

'We might try rocking,' said Gina. 'Give me the keb.'

She took the boat-hook, slid her good leg down on to the gunwale. Then, turning to Mr and Mrs Weaver, she told them where to stand and how to rock when she gave the signal.

'It might work,' she said, 'if the engine's put into reverse at the same time.'

They did precisely as she told them, rocked and stopped rocking, rocked and rocked again. Almost unbelievably there was a movement, and then a loud sucking sound. The mud unwillingly but certainly was releasing the *Marybell*.

'We're off!' cried Timothy. 'Good for you, Gina!' And his parents echoed his praise.

But Gina was only annoyed with herself for having allowed the boat to get stuck in the first place.

They were off the mud bank, it was true, but almost at once the engine seemed slower.

'It's like running a car with the brake on,' said Mr Weaver.

Gina said, 'My guess is you've picked up something.'

'Picked up something?' It sounded like an infection.

' Round the propeller. You'll have to turn the engine off. Just get to your own side again, by the tow-path.'

' You're not telling me I'm going to have to get down into that canal water and fiddle about getting something off the propeller ? What was that I said about peace and quiet on the waterway ? '

Gina smiled.

' My father's been in many a time, but I hope we can manage with the keb, with the boat-hook.'

' So do I,' said Mr Weaver.

Over on his own side, he took the boat-hook and prodded and poked. ' Useful things, these.'

' Yes.'

' There's certainly something there.'

' I wonder what it is,' said Timothy excitedly, lying face down, head over the edge.

' What *could* it be ? ' said Mrs Weaver, anticipating something nice.

' Ha ! ' said Gina, curling her lip. ' Anything nasty.'

' Why nasty ? ' said Timothy, who was looking forward to an exciting discovery.

' When people want to get rid of things, they come down to the Cut. Whoomph ! And a few bubbles. For them that's the end. Easy.'

' But for boat families and holiday-makers out of luck it's the beginning ? ' said Mrs Weaver.

' It costs us time by the hour,' said Gina, sounding middle-aged again.

65

' At least you don't have to worry about time being money today,' said Mrs Weaver. ' Oh, look ! ' She pointed at moorhens that were skittering across flattened reeds. ' Such surprising feet they have ! '

Gina was not concerned at any time with the size or shape or colour of the moorhens' feet. Just now she was only interested in how quickly the obstruction could be removed. But not so Timothy, she was shocked to notice. Even in this predicament he had prised up on his elbows to look at a bird's feet. His father was still busy with the boat-hook.

' Oof ! Done it, I think,' said Mr Weaver. ' Mind yourself, Tim.'

' It's an old sack,' said Timothy, ' tied up. Haul it in, Father, here on deck ! '

' I shouldn't,' said Gina. 'There's no knowing what might be in it.'

' That's what I mean.' There was no mistaking Timothy's excitement. ' It might be something valuable, something stolen that the thief found too dangerous to get rid of.'

His father said, ' You read too many of the wrong sort of stories.'

' It might be a drowned animal,' said his mother, ' and you wouldn't like that. We don't want to know.'

' No,' Gina agreed. ' People don't throw nice things into canals—old tyres, barbed wire, every sort of rubbish, but nothing nice.'

At that second the boat-hook jerked the sack upwards and it went flying across the tow-path. It struck against an iron mileage post, and the old and sodden sacking disintegrated. Timothy's excitement fell away at the sight of the spilled contents.

'Old boots,' he said sadly, 'and old clothes. A tramp's, I suppose.' He groaned.

'I told you so,' said Gina. ''Aul-ups is always rubbish. At best it holds you up. At worst it makes a hole in the boat.'

'You always seem to be right,' said Timothy.

'Only on the Cut. Nowhere else.' Back into her mind came thoughts of the hostel and last night's talk.

But if some things were thrown into the canal, others fell in—or were almost pushed in. Later in the day as the *Marybell* was chugging towards a bend and the canal again seemed a peaceful place, the family was startled by the wild yapping of a dog. Into view came a corgi bounding excitedly after a terrified lamb. The mother sheep was nowhere in sight.

'Look at that dog!' cried Tim. 'Isn't it mean!'

'It's out of hand,' said Gina scornfully.

Faintly, feebly, the dog's devoted owner was calling, 'Hercules, Hercules, come here, you naughty dog!'

But there was no authority in her command, and Hercules, crazy with the chase, paid no heed.

'Call that dog off!' shouted Mr Weaver.

'The lamb will fall in if it isn't careful,' cried

67

Timothy. Even as he spoke, the frenzied creature leapt to escape the corgi and almost somersaulted into the canal.

'It's in, oh, it's gone down! Oh, Father, save it! Stop as soon as you can! We must save it!'

But Gina said, 'Don't go too near in or you'll stick again and you won't save it. Keep there, that's right. You'll need the gang-plank.'

Then unexpectedly, and pretending to throw something, she gave a wild roar at the corgi. The animal turned and became aware at last of its owner. Ashamed now, it almost crawled in her direction and was clipped on the lead. Meanwhile the lamb had risen to the surface and was crying out pathetically.

Mrs Weaver and Timothy were ready with the gang-plank. The second its tip touched the ground Timothy leapt along it and flung himself face down over the canal. With his arm at full length he could just grasp a handful of the lamb's wool at its neck. Then with difficulty, for it was heavy with water, he drew the frantic creature to the edge and gathered it up in his arms.

'There, there, you're safe, safe from the water and safe from the dog. You needn't worry. It won't get you.'

But the lamb's heart was still thumping madly.

Across the field now strode a man who was obviously the farmer. Timothy got to his feet, and with the lamb still cradled, called, 'It isn't dead. It isn't drowned.'

' Thanks to you,' said the farmer warmly as he took the trembling, wet bundle in his arms. ' No thanks at all to that blasted dog or its owner. These late lambs always seem to need special looking after, always find trouble. Not that it should have been in this field, but somebody must have left the gate open.'

He put one hand into his trouser pocket and as the money jingled started to say, ' Take . . .'

' Oh no, no thank you, not for saving something. It's not like getting a reward for finding something.'

' Come along. Take it.'

' No. Honestly, no, thank you.'

' Well, thank you again. Lucky for me you were there.'

' For you ! Lucky for the lamb,' said Timothy, stroking its head.

As he walked back to the boat he tried to imagine what the farmer would say to the dog owner, and what she would say to him.

Later that day the *Marybell* was nearing a lock where ferns sprouted from the joints of the gates, old water-sodden gates. The lengthsman who had cycled by was kneeling at the lock-side, beyond the left gate which was not fully open. He was signalling them on.

' What do we do now, Gina ? What's going on ? '

' There's plenty of room for you,' said Gina, ' but something must be wedged there behind that left gate.'

As soon as the *Marybell* was tied up Mr Weaver ran

over the top gates and down to the lengthsman's side, just as he was starting to haul up a crate with some empty bottles in it. 'Hold on,' called Mr Weaver. 'Let me help you.'

'*Thank* you,' said the lengthsman. 'It's a tidy weight though it's only been in the water a short time.'

'How do you know that?'

'It was stolen, full, from a pub last night by a gang of hooligans, so we were on the look-out this morning. Gates can be badly damaged if they are forced back when there's something wedged behind.'

'And repairs must be awkward to carry out.'

'Costly too. Not to mention the waste of water if there's a break in the woodwork.' Then, turning to Gina, the lengthsman said, 'How do you like a lady's life, eh?' But Gina only smiled and looked shy.

Mr Weaver said, 'She hasn't had much of a rest, between bringing us through the tunnel when the lights failed and getting us off a mud bank.'

'Oh, so that's what's been happening! It was lucky you had her on board then.'

'It was indeed.'

'You must be thinking life's full of excitement on a canal, but it isn't, is it, Gina?'

'No. Mostly nothing happens. We just go on.'

And that is what the *Marybell* did until the Leas' two boats came in sight at dusk that evening.

' I wish you didn't have to go,' said Timothy.

Mr Weaver said, ' It's such a pity you have to leave us before you've met Margaret. Now, here's our address. Don't lose it. If you're ever near our house, come and see us.'

' Yes, do,' said Mrs Weaver.

' If you go to that hostel,' said Timothy, ' you'll learn to write letters. You could send us one.'

' We're going to miss you,' said his mother. ' You've added a lot to the pleasure of our holiday.'

' As well as coming to our rescue.'

Gina said almost nothing, nothing at all about how they had added to the pleasure not merely of those days but of her life, but she thought about it then and later—often, and it gave her a new positiveness, not very noticeable but felt. She had talked to shore people now and enjoyed it ! She had talked about the only thing she knew of—the canal—and they had liked to listen.

6

Gina Talks It Out

When Old Bess saw Gina step back on to the butty, she was almost sprightly with excitement in spite of her years. Hers was the only obvious welcome. Mr Lea was pleased enough to have his daughter back, but he was a silent man. George and Henry took after him.

Mrs Lea said, ' This dog's done nothin' but mope while you've been away. She's taken not the slightest notice of any of us. It's a good job you've come back or she'd 'ave pined away.'

Old Bess repeated her welcome time and again all day. She kept very close to Gina, fussed and wagged and squealed with joy, more like a puppy than a staid old dog.

Gina was glad to see Old Bess, glad to see her family, and yet things seemed different. Day after day, working automatically, she went on with her routine of polishing the brass, peeling potatoes and onions, ' minding ' little Hetty, and, when her ankle got better, swabbing the woodwork on the boat and helping with the locks. But she was restless.

' You don't seem yourself,' said her mother.

' I'm all right.'

' You've never been the same since you were on that *Marybell*. What's the matter with you ? '

' Nothing.'

' I shouldn't have let you go. Didn't they treat you right ? '

' Of course they did.'

' No need to snap my 'ead off. That's not like you either.'

' I'd have told you fast enough if they hadn't been nice to me, but they were extra nice.'

' So they should 'ave been to make up for the fool thing they did.'

Mrs Lea would give shore people credit for nothing. Gina knew it was no use trying to change her attitude.

The trees were almost leafless now. Slowly the days became weeks. In some of the gardens beyond the tow-path red apples gleamed. Autumn leaves were swept and raked into neat heaps on the garden pathways. Under the country trees in the fields they lay where they fell, their colour darkening, their crispness lost in the rain.

And then one day there was fog, not a ribbon of mist like the one Timothy had enjoyed, but an enveloping fog which blotted out the sky, the fields, even the tow-path.

' It's no good,' said Mr Lea, after a miserable hour.

' We shall 'ave to stay tied up.   We can't go any further until this lifts.'

' That's what I was thinkin',' said Mrs Lea.   ' Well, if you'll take the boys with you into the motor, I can have a bit of space in 'ere to make a stew.   Gina'll help me.   You can leave Hetty : she'll sleep on, I dare say, after bein' up last night till eleven.'

Gina settled down to peel parsnips and turnips and onions.   The stove was warm and her eyes began to smart.   ' I hate rain,' she said, sighing, ' but I hate fog even more.'

' We don't get much,' said her mother sharply. ' Whatever's wrong with you this mornin'.   Not sickenin' for anything, are you ? '

' Not that I know of.'

' What then ? '

' Nothing, but I wish we'd kept on longer last night. Then we might have got as far as the depot this morning before the fog thickened.'

' It'll be foggy there too.'   Gina made no reply, so her mother tried again.

' What are you moping about ? '

' I could have had a day at school.'

' Go to school in this fog ?   You must be daft.'

' I miss school.   The weather doesn't matter much when you're at school.   There are bright lights and pictures on the walls, and your dinner laid on, and things to *do* all the time.'

Mrs Lea looked at Gina with disapproval. 'Look at this cabin. I can find you plenty to do here.'

'Yes, Mum, but I've done it all before. It . . . it won't get me anywhere.'

Old Bess, feeling Gina's misery more than Mrs Lea did, snuggled close. Gina patted her but found no comfort for herself.

' " Won't get you nowhere ? " ' Mrs Lea repeated. No reply. Again she tried. ' It's no good boaters 'avin' big ideas. Where d'you want to get ? '

' I don't know,' Gina confessed.

' George and Henry don't make this fuss about gettin' to school. They wouldn't go if I didn't make 'em.'

' Well, they don't care. They're just content to—' and she hesitated.

' To stay ignorant like us, you mean, like your father and me. Nay, you needn't try to deny it. Readin' and writin's not all that much of a catch. What would you do with it ? '

' I don't know, but it would be there. I wouldn't have to take letters to a depot clerk to get them read, that's one thing.'

Mrs Lea looked up from the meat she was cutting, and said, ' Why, you never get letters ! Who's going to write to you ? Oh, I know those Weavers wrote one letter and one picture postcard, but they 'aven't kept it up, 'ave they ? Not likely.'

' They would if I wrote back, but I can't,' said Gina, and the tears that rolled down her cheeks now were not onion tears.

' Oh, dry up ! ' said Mrs Lea, not really unkindly. ' Is that what you're frettin' about ? '

Gina shrugged a shoulder.

Her mother went on : ' Next time we're by Sister

Mary's, I'll ask 'er to write a letter for you, and I'll give you the stamp. 'Ow'll that do ? '

It was meant kindly, but Gina shook her head. ' I want to be able to write my own letters, straight off. I want to be able to read books, long ones, any books, like other people.'

' Like shore people, you mean.'

' Mum,' said Gina, and her voice was imploring, ' I don't want to leave home, even for term-times. It isn't that I want to be away from you, but *let* me go to the hostel.'

' The hostel ! '

If Mrs Lea had been the fainting kind of woman she would have been down on the floor at such an unacceptable, incomprehensible request. Tough as she was, she could not go on at once with what she was doing. She laid down her knife. She could not, she would not believe her ears.

George's whistle outside in the fog almost startled her. His face appeared suddenly, looking clownish with the too-large cap over the uncombed straw-coloured hair.

' Did I leave a spanner on the stove ? ' he said.

His mother did not answer him ; she had something more than spanners to worry about.

' Gina 'ere— ' said Mrs Lea, in a dazed voice. She stopped, and then started again. ' Gina 'ere wants to go to the hostel.'

F

George forgot about the spanner, blundered in, and sat down on the side bed. He pushed his cap back and turned to Gina, finding words at last.

'You must be potty,' he said. Seeing that he got no reply, he said again, 'You must be potty.' Then he added, so he must have wanted to know, for he rarely asked anybody anything, 'What's come over you ? '

'There's nothing sudden about it,' said Gina. ' I only want to be like other people, like ordinary people.'

George said, ' You'd have to go to school every day if you went to the hostel.'

' That's what I want.'

' An' live away fra the boats ? '

' I wouldn't be gone for ever.' Then to her mother she said, ' It's the only way, Mum.'

Mrs Lea, even George could see, was hurt and angry and bewildered, as lost as someone out on a moor might be in that choking fog which swirled slowly in thick white waves beyond the cabin door.

' I've thought about it,' said Gina, sighing. ' I have, for a long time.'

' So that's what you've 'ad on your mind all this time. I knew there was something. We're not good enough for you any more ? '

' I didn't mean that.' Her words were almost a cry. It was causing her deep suffering to be hurting those she loved, and she did love her family.

' You'd come back wi' all sorts o' fancy notions that wouldn't fit in wi' boat life. And that " eddication "— it don't seem to make folk any 'appier as far as I can see.'

' I don't know about that,' said Gina. ' I only know I'll never get the schooling if I don't start now.'

George, slow as a cart-horse, George, who never troubled his head about anything further than the next lock, said, ' You didn't think that out for yourself, I'll bet. It was that Weaver lot pokin' their noses into other folks' business ! '

Gina said nothing. She was afraid to make bad into worse.

Mrs Lea said, ' It's come to somethin', I must say, when my own daughter thinks I can't look after 'er well enough.'

' You can, Mum, you can,' cried Gina, ' quite well enough for a boater's life.'

' You want to get away from it ? '

' What else are you good for ? ' said George.

' I don't know, I don't know, but I want to be able to choose a bit. There may not even be any working boats when I grow up. But even if there are I don't want to be *forced* to work on them. I don't want to be a boatwoman because there's nothing else I can do. Maybe I could work in a canal office, and show holiday folks how to manage their boats. Mum, don't you see ? ' It was an anguished cry.

There was a silence, and then Mrs Lea said, ' 'Ow would I let you go ? The hostel's all right perhaps for families where they've so many children they don't know where to put 'em, but that's not the case wi' us. I can look after my own, thank you, and no 'elp needed.'

Gina was stung to answer, ' But you get help from us. We help on the boats most of the time.'

' Well, and what d'you expect to do ? Sit like ladies and gents all the time and do nothin' ? '

Her voice had grown loud, it seemed even louder, because of the fog that held everything close. Old Bess whimpered : she did not like arguments. Gina's hand crept down to comfort her.

' You don't understand, Mum. You don't understand.'

George said, ' You're not gonna let 'er go to that hostel, Mum ? '

' I thought you came for a spanner,' said Mrs Lea, pointing to where it lay by his feet. Seeing that even George was about to get involved in the argument, she said, ' Get off ! What goes on 'ere is between me and Gina.'

There was a waft of damp air as George opened the cabin doors and let himself out.

' Mum,' said Gina, ' I'll help extra in the holidays if you'll let me go.'

' You wouldn't like it if you got there. You'd 'ave to do as you were told and no mistake. It's so full of rules you'd 'ardly breathe. You wouldn't be free, like you are now.'

Free. That was the word Gina had used when she talked to the Weavers, but she had had time to think since then. Here on the boats she could never make any plans, she never knew where she would be at any particular time, never did anything interesting, or anything different. Mrs Weaver had said, ' I expect you go to the Zoo quite often, as you pass by the very edge of it every few weeks.' But the Leas had never once tied up and taken time off to let their children see the animals. Timothy had found it impossible to understand. It was not that the Leas could not afford it. They had the money, but not the confidence. They were not comfortable mixing with, being noticed by, shore people as they felt they would be at the Zoo. And to make the effort for the sake of their children was something they did not understand.

It was not until Gina met the Weavers that she realized she knew practically nothing about the places near the canal. All her life she had travelled up and down it. All her life, but it was *they*, the mere visitors to the Cut, who told *her* nice titbits about the towns and villages, and they had found it all in books. They knew what there was over the railway-line. Gina had gone on remembering that. And a train line wasn't just a train line. They knew about the invention of steam engines and everything.

' I'd like to try the hostel, Mum,' she said.

' Well, we'll see.' Gina was silent, scarcely believing she was hearing aright. ' But no comin' back with big ideas, no tellin' us 'ow to behave or which knives and spoons to use, like some I've 'eard of. The ideas you pick up on the shore you keep for the shore, understand ? '

' Yes, Mum. Oh, thank you. Thank you.'

But Mrs Lea brushed aside the thanks.

' We are as we are, and we shan't change, bein' boaters on both sides of the family far back. You've always been just that bit different. I don't know whether it's for good or ill.'

Gina suddenly felt very tired. Never in her life had she had such a long conversation with her mother. For the most part there was nothing to talk about. Just when all seemed settled in Gina's mind, her mother pointed to Old Bess.

' What about 'er if you go ? '

Gina felt stopped in her tracks. Faintly she said, ' I hadn't thought about her.'

' I thought you 'adn't. You were only thinkin' of yourself.'

' I'd come back in the holidays.'

' Bess wouldn't know that. She'd pine away long before then.'

' But you'd come and see me whenever you were up, wouldn't you ? Every three weeks or so.'

' We would, but they wouldn't 'ave a dog in a place like that.'

But Gina had an answer for that too.

' I would come out with you, Mum, with you and Old Bess.'

' W-ell, maybe, but I can't see 'er lastin' long if you go. You've always been her favourite. I've never seen a dog sorrow as she did when you were with those shore people, and that was a short time. She was somethin' pitiful. Go if you like, but I can't promise Old Bess'll be 'ere when you get back.'

And Gina's hopes fell away. She raised her eyes to the horse brasses that were already dulled by the seeping fog.

' I can't let Old Bess suffer,' she said bleakly, finally, flatly, and in despair. Kneeling, she sobbed into Old Bess's tattered coat.

' She's always looked after you,' said her mother, twisting the knife in the potato.

And both knew she would always look after Old Bess. Twelve years is a long time. The habit was too hard to break. Mrs Lea, with Old Bess as her final card, had won.

7

Old Bess's Night

The autumn changed to winter, and it was a hard one. Sometimes the Leas had to break the ice on the canal before they could start off in the morning.

Nothing much happened. One day in the dusk a low bough caught the chimney of the butty and sent it crashing down the steps into the cabin. Another day a stray length of rope wrapped itself round the blades of the propeller, and it was a full hour's work to get it off. A tremendous storm broke, and lightning struck a tree not far from the pair of boats. When the noise of thunder was over the rain continued, lashing on the boats, forcing its way in though the hatch was closed. Tins and bowls were placed here and there to catch the drips which came ' pinging ' in, hour after hour.

There were mornings of beauty, too, when every bush stood decked with frost, and icicles hung from roof and railing. Mornings of beauty for the shore people, but for the boaters there were icy ropes to untie and slippery lock steps to climb.

Gina's life continued as always. There had been no

more talk of the hostel. It was as though the subject had never been mentioned.

Just after the turn of the year Old Bess became ill. All the family, even little Hetty who could barely talk, waited on her. After a time, so desperate were they that they stopped off at the next town, wrapped her in the old coat she slept on and carried her to a vet. Never had they gone to a vet with any other animal, but they took time off for Old Bess and let the load wait. Time might be money, but it did not seem to matter as much as usual. Mr Lea carried her, and his wife and all his children followed, a cheerless procession through the dreary streets.

' Do you think she'll ever get better ? ' Gina whispered.

' Sh ! ' said her father. ' The vet will know what to do, you'll see.' But that was his hope rather than his belief.

The vet examined Old Bess carefully while all the family stood and watched and waited. Then he straightened his back.

' There is nothing, I regret, nothing at all I can do. I only wish I could save her.'

' She's not going to die,' said Gina, daring him to say it.

' I'm afraid she is, and you mustn't sorrow. She's

85

had a very long life for a dog, you know. Do you want to leave her here ? Would it help you ? '

Leave her with a stranger ! Leave her there to die !

That they would not do. They wrapped Old Bess again in the old coat and carried her tenderly home. At eleven o'clock that January night, quietly she died.

The boats were moored only yards away from Sister Mary's house. They and the buildings shone silver in the light of the full moon, but the air was icy cold and the wind moaned through the bare trees.

Sister Mary was already upstairs for the night when she thought she heard the noise of crying children. She drew back her curtain. Yes, there was a beam of light from a moored boat.

In a minute she was downstairs and putting on her cape. It was lucky that she fastened it at the neck, for as she left the house the wind snatched it and swept it in the air. She struggled and gathered it about her as she walked over the gates to the mooring-bay on the other side of the water.

The Leas heard her distinctive tap on the side of the boat, and one and all were glad of it. The doors were opened in a flash, and she saw at once the cause of their crying.

' I'm not surprised you're upset, my poor dears,' she said, ' but remember the good things. Old Bess couldn't have had a kinder family all these years—how many is it ? Ten ? Eleven ? '

'Twelve,' said Gina and George and Henry, as if with one voice.

'Well then! She couldn't live for ever, you know.'

'It isn't that, Sister Mary, but . . .' and Gina's tears welled up again, 'my dad won't keep her on the boat till morning.'

Mr Lea looked as troubled as anybody, but he said firmly, 'It wouldn't be right, Sister Mary. I couldn't 'ave a dead dog on board all night. That's what all the fuss is about.'

Mrs Lea said, 'My husband is going to wrap 'er up and put her under the hedge until mornin'.'

At that the crying burst out again. Little Hetty's eyes had a wan, hollow look in her thin face.

Sister Mary said, 'If you make all that noise, you won't hear what I have to say.' Immediately they quietened. 'Now, my idea is this, and I'm sure it will make everybody feel more content. Let's give Old Bess a funeral now.'

'This time o' night, Sister Mary? Why, it must be gettin' on for midnight.'

'Well, unless something's done it doesn't look as though there's going to be peaceful sleep for anybody.'

There was sense in that. There always was sound sense in what Sister Mary said.

'But the ground'll be hard, Sister Mary, and I haven't a spade.'

'Never you mind. I have two, and a pick, and a

87

lantern, and I know just the place in the paddock. You couldn't have a prettier corner. In a few weeks there will be hazel catkins, and then primroses. The children can help me, though I expect you'd like to keep Hetty here.'

Sister Mary turned from Mrs Lea to her husband. She had known them both when they were little, and all their lives since.

' You just carry Old Bess, wrapped in her coat, over to the paddock, and then you can come back and leave the rest to me.'

' Yes, Sister Mary,' said Mr Lea, glad to take orders from her.

' We'll call at the house, the boys will take the spades, and Gina shall carry the lantern.'

' Yes, Sister Mary.'

Gina picked up something and slipped it in her pocket. Then, without a word, she stepped ashore. None of them was crying any more. They were almost cheerful. There was something important to do, and Sister Mary would see them through it.

Then Hetty realized that she was to be left behind, and her great bellow of protest startled an owl and sent it winging across the moon.

Mrs Lea said, ' Will you let 'er come, Sister Mary ? She was that fond of Old Bess. She'll only worry and wonder what's goin' on.'

' If you really want it then. Henry, you're in charge

of her. Don't let go of her hand across the gates.'

' No, Sister Mary,' said Henry, tenderly muffling Hetty in an enormous scarf.

It was a strange procession in the moonlight over the great gates above the black and silver water—Mr Lea carrying Old Bess, George and Henry with Hetty between them, then Gina, and last of all Sister Mary with her white head-dress almost floating, casting a magic over the night.

Only when they reached the chosen place in the paddock did Henry loosen his hold on Hetty's small, cold hand.

' Stand there,' he said. ' Don't you move. I've got some diggin' to do.'

' Me too,' said the little one.

' No,' said George, ' there's only two spades.'

' And much too big and heavy for you,' Henry added.

Sister Mary said, ' You can hold the lantern, Hetty. Here, rest it on this tree stump, and just hold the handle. That will be a great help.'

And Hetty was satisfied.

Gina said, ' There's nothing for me now that she's got the lantern, Sister Mary.'

' Indeed there is, but we shall have to go to the house to make it. There certainly is something you can do for this occasion. Come now.'

As they went across the paddock Sister Mary said, ' First, ask your mother to have some cocoa ready.

They'll be glad to have something hot to come back to. And a few nice biscuits would bring a bit of cheer.'

It was difficult for George and Henry to dig a hollow in the hard ground. By the time they had finished George said, ' I'm warm now. I feel better than I did too.'

' Me too,' said Henry. ' I'm glad we were near Sister Mary's. I wonder what Sister Mary and Gina are up to.'

' Comin',' said Hetty, pointing.

' Oh yes. What's Gina carryin' ? ' said George.

' I can't see,' said Henry.

When Gina came close she said, ' It's a cross. I made it. Two pieces of wood and a nail. And look on this board. No, don't touch, Hetty, the paint is wet. Look, *two words*—Old Bess. I painted them.'

The boys looked at her in admiration.

' They're nice,' said George.

' Nice,' said Henry.

George was very impressed by all that was going on. ' You've turned it into a proper funeral, Sister Mary.'

Henry nodded.

Gently Sister Mary laid Old Bess, still in the coat, down in the hollow. Gina fumbled in her pocket and then bent low, putting something in the ground.

In surprise Henry said, ' Did you bring her something too ? '

' Her ball,' said Gina. ' She liked to have it even

when she didn't play with it.   What have you got ? '

Not at all shyly but as though used to such affairs Henry placed Old Bess's drinking bowl beside her.

' That was very thoughtful of you both,' said Sister Mary.

Then she saw George adding the collar and lead. Little Hetty saw him too and knew something was going on in which she had no part.

' Me, me ! ' she said, her voice piercing clear in the silent night.

So George unclipped the lead and gave the collar to Hetty.

' Here you are, you can put that in for Old Bess.'

' Why ? ' said Hetty, in the way she often did now.

' I don't rightly know,' said George, ' but it wants doin', so are you a-goin' to do it or am I ? '

Hetty was not going to miss her chance.   She darted from the lantern, popped in the collar, and darted back again, content.

' That's right,' said Gina.   ' Bess is going on a long journey, and she'll need a few things of her own about her.'

George and Henry shovelled the earth into place and replaced the turf.   Gina fixed the cross firmly and leaned the head-board against it.

' And now,' said Sister Mary, ' we'll say a little prayer.'

They put their hands together and bowed their heads

and listened. Precisely as Sister Mary finished the prayer, the clock on the village church struck one.

As they all walked back across the paddock, Sister Mary said, 'It's very late now, later than you've ever been to bed before, I think, but you can all go to sleep content. Everything has been attended to, remember

that, and you've done it all beautifully. I'm very proud
of you. Good night, my children.'

' Good night, Sister Mary.'

' You will sleep well, all of you.'

And it was as she said. It always was as Sister Mary
said.

G

8

The Hostel

January passed, and February, and the hazel catkins
came. Early in March the boats went into the depot.
The engine had been giving trouble for several days.
When Mr Lea came back to the butty, he said, ' It's goin'
to take a week, so I've been given some painting to do.
And you, Gina, will get a week at school.'

George said, ' Oh good, not me and Henry.'

' Yes, you and Henry too, but I knew Gina'd be the
only one who'd be pleased at the news.'

Henry said, ' Don't send us. We 'aven't gotta go,
'ave we, Mum ? '

' That you 'ave. What would I do with you under
my feet all day long 'ere ? '

Henry said, ' You don't say that when we're on the
move and lock-wheelin' and gettin' water for you an'
everythin'.'

' One more word out of you ! ' said his mother, but
Henry had skipped neatly on to the shore, not because
he was wrong. His parents, without even thinking
about it, did expect and get service from their children

at almost all hours of the day. Gina was aware of that more clearly than the boys were, but she knew their mother and father loved them for themselves too.

' We shall get 'ot dinners any'ow,' said George to Henry, as they moved out of hearing. ' That's one thing.'

Gina liked the dinners too, but for her school meant more than that. A week at school ! She felt nearly gay. She wished it could be a month, six months, a year.

A few days later Mr Lea said, ' There's more to do than they thought. The repair's goin' to take a fortnight.'

The boys groaned. Gina said nothing, but Mrs Lea saw her eyes light up.

' There's one who isn't sorry,' she said.

Gina almost said how much she wished she could go to school every day, but somehow she could never start properly on the subject of the hostel again. Not for lack of courage only. The strife within her kept her silent.

Looking back, Mrs Lea could not imagine how on that one occasion in the fog she had almost let herself be persuaded. If there hadn't been Old Bess, Gina might have got near going, but it had all been a whim and fancy. She must have been mad, she told herself, even to have listened. She wasn't having a child of hers go away ! Once they'd gone you'd lost them, she

argued, to herself and other people. They weren't yours if you handed them over to other folks who'd bring them up differently. She talked about it to her husband while the older children were at school and Hetty was having a sleep.

' I expect it was just a passin' fancy, after bein' with that Weaver family,' said Mr Lea. ' They weren't bad, but they weren't our kind. I never 'ear Gina mention the hostel, so it must 'ave all worn off.'

' I've mentioned the hostel,' said Mrs Lea, ' but only to run it down, you can be sure. I don't want 'er to feel she's missed somethin', and I want 'er to think she decided against it 'erself.'

After a fortnight at school Gina's teacher said, ' In this *short* time I can see you've improved.'

Gina blushed and said, ' It's seemed a lovely long time to me.'

' If only you were at school every day you would learn very fast.'

With that encouragement Gina's words came pouring out. She told her teacher all about the talk there had been that far-off day in the fog, about the Weavers too and how they had read aloud, about her mother and how she had seemed nearly to have agreed to Gina's going away.

' What stopped it then ? ' said the teacher. ' Why was it that you didn't go ? '

' My mum put a spoke in the wheel. She said Old Bess would pine away and be dead when I came back. So I couldn't go, could I ? I should have—well, caused it, shouldn't I ? It was true. She was my dog more than anybody's.'

The teacher let her go on until she finished. It wasn't often a canal child talked at such length.

' But now, Gina, there isn't Old Bess to hold you back. Is there something else to stop you now ? '

' W—ell,' said Gina in a hopeless sort of way, ' she's against it now, my mum. Whenever she says anything it's to put me off, somebody being ticked off by the matron or at school, somebody leaving because they don't like it. I might not like it either. If I didn't, she'd never leave off saying that I'd brought it on myself.'

' That's a risk you'd have to take, and I don't think it would happen,' said the teacher. ' You'd get a lot out of being at the hostel, Gina, as well as out of attending a school every day. You've got it in you to do well, and you have courage. Of course, being with children who started school at five, you'd have to work hard.'

' I wouldn't mind that, but I daren't start it all up again, I daren't,' said the girl.

Then the teacher said something which had not occurred to Gina.

She said, ' Well, it would be a pity to do it for nothing. There may not be room at the hostel, even if your mother agrees to let you go. It isn't any good upsetting yourself and your parents if there is a long waiting-list. I'll see what I can find out.'

So Gina said nothing at home, and by Monday morning the boats were away again. More helping with the locks, more polishing, potato peeling, more putting up the brass rails—the 'nipper' rails—which were meant to stop Hetty from falling overboard. More sameness, and yet not quite such dull sameness, for the spring was very near—and, besides, something was being found out. Gina looked forward to the end of the round trip which would bring her back to school again. She could wait that time more or less content.

But she did not need, as it happened, to wait so long. When they got to the docks at the other end of their journey, there was a message waiting for Mrs Lea.

Another boater came along to bring it. He was a man who had worked for ten years on the Cut. To the Leas who had spent a lifetime on it he seemed almost like a beginner. His wife was a real boater, born to the life, but he was still more like one of the shore folk—according to Mr and Mrs Lea.

'Message for you,' he said. 'The matron of the hostel has been down. She'd like to see you, Mrs Lea, or both of you if you can manage it.'

Gina held her breath. What was happening? Had her teacher written to Matron? Or telephoned all that way?

Mrs Lea said, ' She's nothin' to see me for.   What's it about ? '

' Well, it seems she has three vacancies—room for three more at the hostel.'

' So she thinks she's gonna get Gina and the boys, does she ?   Not likely.   Whatever would we do without their 'elp ? '

' Oh, you'll " do " all right,' said the man.   ' She didn't mention George and Henry.   She's offered my girl a place because she fancies school, always has, so we've said we'll let her have her chance.   We wouldn't want her to say later that we'd stood in her way.'

Mrs Lea was slow to answer.   She could feel Gina's eyes upon her.   It was that last sentence which had made her pause—' We wouldn't want her to say later that we'd stood in her way.'   Put like that, she did not want to stand in her children's way, or sometimes she didn't, but she could not talk about it.

All she said was, ' Who's the other place for ? '

The boater jerked his thumb towards a family that stood further along in a little huddle.   They were talking anxiously, and looking round to see that no one else was near enough to hear.

' They're that crowded,' said the boater, ' one has to sleep on the floor.   They were told they'd have to leave the boats or let one of their children go to the hostel.   That's what all the talk's about.'

' It's not like that with us,' said Mrs Lea belligerently.

' We've got room enough for all ours to sleep.'

' It's not just the present time we have to think of. We're concerned for our girl's future. The boats can't last, you know.'

Fiercely for him, Mr Lea said, ' Are you telling me we're a dying race ? '

' I've no wish to start an argument. I'm just not wanting my child to grow up feeling a stranger in her own country. She's skilled with a boat, but what else ? Now's the time to learn. It'll be harder later.'

The boater looked at Gina, who looked away, troubled. She did not know what was going to happen. She did not know for certain now what she wanted to happen, but here was a boater—one brought up on the shore—saying much what Mrs Weaver had said. Gina remembered her every word, and cherished the thought of the future Mrs Weaver had drawn for her.

The man said, ' I think it got around some time back that Gina wanted to go to school regular, and Matron's heard she has brains and only needs a chance to use them—a chance she can't get in the sort of life we lead.'

Mrs Lea felt anger and pride all at once, anger that any boat people should know Gina wanted to go away, and pride that a child of hers was thought to have ' brains '. She drew herself up.

' If Matron wants Gina, she'll 'ave to come and see me. I'm not usin' any shoe leather traipsin' about.'

' Oh, she's coming here all right if you don't go

there. She knew you'd be in today and said she counted on your not going out tonight because she'd be down.'

' We 'ad a mind to go to the pictures,' said Mrs Lea, 'and I don't see why we should make any changes. Gina's given up this nonsense about the hostel.'

' W—ell,' said the boater, watching Gina blink the tears back, ' it doesn't look like it.'

Fiercely Mrs Lea said, ' Open your mouth, child ! Tell him you've changed your mind. You have changed it, haven't you ? '

Now was the moment. Gina knew there would be no other, and just now the other boater was there and on her side. If she wanted to fit herself for any other sort of life, she must speak now.

She swallowed, and in a hard little voice that did not sound like hers she said, ' No, I haven't changed my mind.'

It was a stormy evening—stormy weather outside the boat and inside it, but gradually the storms died down. As Matron talked it seemed more right that Gina should go to the hostel. Matron too stressed the future, and the opportunities that could not be taken unless one learned to read usefully and to write.

In the next two days Gina was full of hopes and doubts and fears which jostled one against the other. Gradually there were more hopes than fears, and Matron got

round Mrs Lea—enough at least for Gina to change
from boat to hostel in—well, not in peace exactly, but
not in an atmosphere of family war.

Looking back, Gina would always remember that
first night in the hostel, the first night in her life when
she had not slept on a boat.

She lay there looking up at the ceiling which seemed
so far away. From time to time beams of light from
outside moved across it.

The other children in the dormitory were fast asleep
when Matron came in.

At Gina's bed-side she smiled and whispered, ' Off
you go to sleep now, Gina. It's a new day tomorrow,
and you're going to enjoy it. Good night now.'

' Good night, Matron.'

As Matron walked away towards the door, Gina
realized that the floor had not moved. It was perfectly
still, and there was no creaking of mooring-ropes. Such
a large room it seemed to her, and airy, with big windows.
Even if it rained the windows could stay open and the
rain would not come in, and that was nice, better than
a hatch which had to be closed when the rain began—
unless you were prepared for the floor of the cabin to be
slopping wet.

All sorts of things had been nice that evening, thought
Gina—the chatter of the children round a big supper
table with knives and spoons laid out on it, the sight of
Matron's reassuring face, the all-over warmness after

a bath. Gina lifted her arm to her face: she could still smell the soap.

She smiled in the darkness as she remembered the rush of water when she pulled the lavatory chain. For a second only she had thought it was water rushing into a lock. But the school lavatories had been proper ones too, in that new building where the boat children felt they had no right to be, even in the rooms set aside for them. That ' not belonging ' was finished for Gina now. The canal school stayed open nearly all the year round, so in the next holidays she would go back to see her teacher. If the boats were sold, and the rumour was getting stronger, there would be no canal school. Where would her teacher go then ? Those words, ' You've got it in you to do well, and you have courage '.

She moved her feet and found enjoyment in the smooth coolness of the sheets. They were part of this new life. Sheets on a bed, and a bed of proper shape and size. Room to turn over. She was wearing pyjamas too ; they belonged to the hostel but they were hers to wear. Not that they were as pretty as those she had worn on the *Marybell*. Before long, if she tried hard, she would be able to write to her shore family. Perhaps she would even see them again one day. She had a toothbrush now, and a tube of toothpaste. It would be nice to put out her hand and touch them, but the effort was just too great.

Sleep had come.